NAME THE GREATEST OF ALL THE INVENTORS: ACCIDENT.

—*Mark Twain*

TO JON,
WITH LOVE

First U.S. edition 2019

Library of Congress Catalog Card Number pending
ISBN 978-1-5362-0271-7

18 19 20 21 22 23 WKT 10 9 8 7 6 5 4 3 2 1

Printed in Shenzhen, Guangdong, China

This book was typeset in Edbaskerville.
The illustrations were created digitally.

Nosy Crow
an imprint of
Candlewick Press
99 Dover Street
Somerville, Massachusetts 02144

www.nosycrow.com
www.candlewick.com

DAVE'S ROCK

FRANN PREST-N-GANNON

nosy crow™

An imprint of Candlewick Press

This Dave.

Dave **love** rock.

Jon **love** rock, too.

Dave's rock **bigger.**

Jon's rock **faster.**

Dave find
new rock.

New rock
prettier.

Dave's rock
not rock.

Jon's rock **taller.**

Dave **not** happy . . .

but
Jon have
idea!

Jon make rock **better**.

Dave make rock **better**, too.

Look! Rocks same. Nice and round.
Matching rocks give Dave idea!

Dave find stick.
Rocks make fun game!

Jon and Dave **happy.**

Friends happy, too.